D1007310

MOTHER
Knows Best

by **Sarah Willson**

illustrated by **Robert Dress**

Simon Spotlight/Nickelodeon

New York   London   Toronto   Sydney

Based on the TV series *SpongeBob SquarePants*®
created by Stephen Hillenburg as seen on Nickelodeon®

SIMON SPOTLIGHT
An imprint of Simon & Schuster Children's Publishing Division
1230 Avenue of the Americas, New York, New York 10020

Manufactured in the United States of America

6 8 10 9 7

ISBN-13: 978-1-4169-0793-0
ISBN-10: 1-4169-0793-9

Library of Congress Catalog Card Number 2005002983

1211RR6

Look for these other
SpongeBob SquarePants
chapter books!

chapter one

"Ahhhh!" said SpongeBob, breathing in deeply as he stepped out of his front door. "What a super-sailoriffic-sunshiney day!" he said to no one in particular. The sun was shining, the water shimmering, and the scallops were chirping.

"Hmm," said SpongeBob, stopping halfway down the path. "I have a funny feeling I've forgotten to do something." SpongeBob thought hard.

Then he brightened. "Oh, yes! I almost forgot to call my mother to tell her I love her!"

He hurried back inside and dialed his mother's phone number.

"Hi, Mom," he said. "I was just about to leave for work when I remembered I hadn't called you today. Are you still proud of me? You are? Oh, good! Well, I just wanted to say"—SpongeBob's eyes welled up with tears, and his voice started to wobble—"thanks for being the world's best mom! I love you."

His mother said something into the phone.

"No, I love *you* more!"

She said something else.

"No, I love *you* even more!"

This conversation continued for several more minutes. SpongeBob made one final vow as to how deeply he loved his mother, and then he set off for the Krusty Krab.

"Good morning, SpongeBob!" called SpongeBob's best friend, Patrick Star. "Off to work?"

"Yes, I am, Patrick!" SpongeBob replied heartily. "It's a beautiful day, I have a terrific job, and most importantly I have . . ." His

voice wobbled again. "I have a mother who loves me! What more could I ask for?"

"Uh . . . maybe a lifetime supply of ice cream?" Patrick wondered, scratching his head.

"No, Patrick, a mother's love is all that matters," said SpongeBob before heading to work.

SpongeBob was lost in thought as he walked along the edge of a deep trench. "Mother's Day is coming up soon," he said to himself. "I have to give Mom something really, *really* special. Maybe I'll make something for her. After all, she's made me who I am to—" SpongeBob suddenly stopped. Was that the sound of someone crying?

Someone was sitting at the edge of the trench with his head buried in his arms and his knees drawn up to his chest. He was sniffling loudly. SpongeBob had passed right by him.

He hurried back and asked, "What's the matter, mister?"

The man looked up at SpongeBob, his eyes red with tears. "I'm having trouble at work," he said flatly. "If I lose my job, life will be meaningless."

SpongeBob was surprised: How could anyone be so unhappy when he himself was so happy? While it was true that not everyone could rise to the level of fry cook at

the Krusty Krab as he had done, surely there was something in this man's life that made him happy?

"Oh, sir, there must be something good in your life," said SpongeBob.

The man shook his head, then took SpongeBob's tie and blew his nose on it loudly. "My job means everything to me. But I made some bad decisions and now everyone at work is mad at me!"

"Now, now," said SpongeBob, patting him on the shoulder. Then an idea occurred to him. "Do you . . . do you have a mother?" he asked the man.

The man shrugged, then nodded.

"Well, then, think of how lucky you are!" declared SpongeBob. He stood up and put a hand on his chest. "While it may be true that you're having trouble with your job, and you're afraid you're going to be fired, and you'll never work in this town again . . ."

With each thing SpongeBob named, the man's shoulders slumped lower and lower. Suddenly he burst into tears.

"Wait, sir," said SpongeBob hastily, "what I'm trying to say is that no matter what else may be going wrong in your life, at least you know that you have a mother's love! And no one can take *that* away from you!"

Hearing SpongeBob's words, the man shook himself, as though waking from a dream.

His face brightened as he scrambled to his feet.

"Wow!" he said, thrusting out a hand. "That was an inspiring speech. A mother's love! Of course! I *do* have that!"

He shook SpongeBob's hand. SpongeBob smiled. "Well, I guess I should be on my way," said SpongeBob.

"I was feeling blue because my TV station's ratings have gone down," explained the man. "You see, I am a producer of television shows. Recently I hired some people to host shows, and they were, uh, poor choices. No one watches the shows, and the people who pay for the shows are mad at me! But none of that matters! Thanks to you, I realize that I do have a mom who loves me no matter how bad my ratings are!"

"Ah, that's great," said SpongeBob as he

started to walk away. But the man clapped him on the shoulder. "Wait," he said. "I would like to offer you a job!"

Before SpongeBob could tell him that he already had the world's best job, the man continued. "My name is Sam Sandollar. Your speech was so heartwarming, so empowering, I see real talent in you, and I am an excellent judge of talent. Would you like to host your own television show? You can start right away!"

SpongeBob's eyes widened. "My—my own TV show? Wow!"

"Here's my card," said Sam. "I'll see you in my office this afternoon!"

chapter two

SpongeBob ran into Mr. Krabs's office as soon as he got to the Krusty Krab.

"Mr. Krabs! Mr. Krabs!" he yelled. Mr. Krabs was counting his money, and was so startled that he threw a pile of bills into the air.

"Ya scared me pants off me, SpongeBob!"

he said, scooping up the bills. "What's all the ruckus?"

"I wanted you to be the first to hear," said SpongeBob, talking so fast he could barely get the words out. "I'm going to be a star! A TV guy offered me my own TV show!"

Squidward poked his head into the office to see what all the fuss was about. He snorted. "You? Your own show? Puh-leeze."

"I know, it's amazing, isn't it?" said SpongeBob.

"What's the show about?" asked Squidward.

"Uh, gee. I'm not sure," said SpongeBob, looking puzzled. Then he grinned. "But I'm sure it's going to be great!"

"I'm proud of you, SpongeBob, me boy," said Mr. Krabs, putting a claw on SpongeBob's shoulder. "You have fun with that show . . . as long as it happens on your own time!"

"Oh, yes," said SpongeBob. "I forgot to mention that. It looks like I'll have to quit my job, Mr. Krabs. Hosting my own show is a full-time job. But don't worry. Even if you don't find someone to replace me right away, everything will be fine! The most important thing is that you have a mother who loves you!"

"Barnacles! What does me mum have to do with anything!" thundered Mr. Krabs. "Ya can't quit now, boy! Mother's Day is two weeks away, and we're going to be swamped! I'm having a special Mother's Day menu! Same food, double the prices! I need you to work!"

But SpongeBob was already unclipping his name tag and placing his hat neatly on the desk. "I'm sorry, Mr. Krabs," he said, looking very regretful. "You know I love being a fry cook more than anything in the world. But this is the opportunity of a lifetime. Thanks for everything."

And SpongeBob walked out the door.

Mr. Krabs was in shock.

"Don't worry, Mr. Krabs. He'll be back," said Squidward. "The show is sure to bomb. It's not like he knows how to do anything besides make Krabby Patties. I give him one day and he'll be right back at the fry station." Squidward chuckled gleefully at the thought.

SpongeBob headed toward the TV studio.

"Hey, SpongeBob, where are you going?" asked Patrick. He was standing at the ice-cream truck buying a strawberry ice-cream cone. "I thought you were on your way to work!"

"I *am* on my way to work, Patrick!" said SpongeBob. "I have a new job! I'm going to be the star of my own television show!"

"Can I be on it?" asked Patrick.

"First I have to find out what it's about!" said SpongeBob.

When SpongeBob arrived at the studio, he was immediately taken to a huge conference room. Sitting around a long table were about two dozen serious-looking executives. They stared at SpongeBob. Just as SpongeBob was starting to feel a tiny bit nervous, the man he had met that morning came flying into the room and put his arm around SpongeBob's shoulders. "Here he is, folks, the guy I told you about!" he said to the executives.

"These are my disgruntled advertising sponsors," he said to SpongeBob in a low voice. "They're not happy with the hosts I hired. But don't let them make you nervous.

We have moms who are proud of us, remember?"
He winked at SpongeBob.

The clock ticked loudly as no one said anything. SpongeBob smiled shyly, but didn't dare say a word.

Finally one of the executives spoke. "You think this—this *sponge* can host a live show

about cooking, cleaning tips, knitting, quilting, crafting, and child care? You think that *he* will be able to give members of our studio audience homespun advice?"

"The last one he hired tripped on her yarn and broke her arm," muttered another executive.

"And the one before that couldn't even make toast. She nearly burned the studio to the ground," said a third.

"Didn't we decide we needed a *mother* to host the show?" asked another. "After all, the show *is* called *Mother Knows Best.*"

Sam Sandollar waved his hand as if to dismiss all doubts. "He's perfect!" he assured them. "And I'll tell you why. Although he's not exactly a mother himself, he *does* have a mother. And she *loves* him. Right, SpongeBob?" he said, turning

to SpongeBob and patting him on the back.

"Uh, right!" said SpongeBob, after he had stopped coughing.

"Great! Then the first show will air tomorrow!" said Sam Monroe.

There was a good deal of grumbling as the meeting ended.

Back home SpongeBob found Patrick, Squidward, and even Mr. Krabs waiting for him.

"How did it go?" asked Patrick.

"Great!" said SpongeBob. "I'm going to do a show about cooking, cleaning tips, knitting, quilting, crafts, and child care! And I'm going to give members of the studio audience homespun advice!"

"Ha! Ha! Ha!" snorted Squidward. "Did you hear that, Mr. Krabs? SpongeBob is supposed to be an expert at that stuff? Him? Ha! Ha! . . . Huh?"

Squidward stopped laughing. He had just noticed SpongeBob holding a set of knitting needles, which were moving so fast they were a blur. A long wool scarf was growing rapidly beneath his hands.

"Here, Patrick," said SpongeBob, wrapping the scarf around his friend's neck. "I thought I heard you cough a moment ago. This should protect you from drafts and help you feel better."

"Gee, thanks, SpongeBob," said Patrick gratefully, going over to the mirror to admire his new scarf.

Squidward watched, amazed as SpongeBob snapped open his sewing-machine case, flipped on the machine, and expertly fed thread through the needle. Then the sewing machine began to whir, and in the blink of an eye a beautiful quilt appeared.

Ding!

An oven timer had gone off. Squidward and Mr. Krabs watched, openmouthed, as SpongeBob hurried over to the oven and pulled out three perfect cake layers.

"Ah! Another perfect cake," said SpongeBob, dusting off his floury hands on his apron. "Just like my mother taught me!" he added.

Squidward and Mr. Krabs were dumbfounded.

"Well, he certainly doesn't know the first thing about dealing with kids, that's for sure!" muttered Squidward to Mr. Krabs.

Crash! A baseball suddenly burst through the window, shattering it. The ball rolled up to SpongeBob's feet.

SpongeBob picked it up. "What are those mischievous rascals up to now?" he said, chuckling as he walked over to the front door.

"Gee, we're so sorry about that, Mr. SpongeBob," said the two kids standing on the doorstep with a baseball bat.

"Oh, don't worry, kids!" said SpongeBob, patting them on their heads and handing them back the ball. "Kids will be kids, right? Here, have a freshly baked cookie. And then run along home and tell your mother how much you love her!"

"Thanks, Mr. SpongeBob," said one of the kids. "You're the best!"

Squidward looked at Mr. Krabs and shrugged. "Who knew?" he said.

chapter three

SpongeBob's show was a smash hit. *Everyone* in Bikini Bottom watched it. A few mornings after the show had begun, SpongeBob stepped out of his limo in front of the studio. A huge crowd was there cheering for their new TV star.

"Thanks for watching. Thanks for watching. Thanks for watching," said SpongeBob as he walked past the crowd.

"Hi, SpongeBob!" yelled Patrick, jumping up and down and waving wildly.

But SpongeBob barely looked his way. "Hey, thanks," he said. "Thanks for watching."

As SpongeBob started to walk inside, Patrick grabbed him.

"Excuse *me*, Mr. SpongeBob Superior Pants!" he said. "Aren't you forgetting who your friends are?"

SpongeBob started to reply when an assistant rushed up and handed him a note. "From your mother, Mr. SpongeBob," she said breathlessly. SpongeBob opened it up.

Dear SpongeBob,

   I am so proud of you! You are doing a great job on your show! Just don't forget to be nice to your friends. Friends are very important in life, after all.

Your Loving Mother

SpongeBob looked up from the note and sighed, his eyes shining. "That mother of mine is always so wise!" he said. Then he noticed Patrick, as though for the first time. He threw his arms around his friend.

"Patrick, Patrick, I am sorry I didn't pay enough attention to you!" he said. "You're my best friend, and friends are very important, right? Huh, pal?"

Patrick nodded as best he could while being squeezed around the head. "Yeah, I guess that's true," he said in a muffled voice.

"Come on in!" said SpongeBob. "You can watch today's show from a front-row seat. The subject is Cake Decorating."

"And that," said SpongeBob at the end of the show, "is how to create a perfect frosted flower." He was busily piping pink roses all around the edges of a towering frosted cake. The audience oohed and ahhed.

"Questions?" asked SpongeBob, leaping into the audience and thrusting a microphone under someone's chin.

"How did you learn to make such perfect cakes?" a lady asked.

"Well," said SpongeBob, modestly polishing his knuckles, "I owe it all to one person: my mom."

"Awwwwww," said the audience.

Another person asked, "I want to knit a sweater for my husband. He's a hammerhead shark and hard to fit. Any advice for me, SpongeBob?"

"Try a roll-neck collar!" SpongeBob replied. "It tends to be looser than ribbing at the neckline."

The audience cheered as the closing music began to play. Sam Sandollar dashed out of the control room and raced over to SpongeBob.

"Another fantastic show, SpongeBob!" he said. "That mother of yours sure did raise a dynamite kid!"

"Thanks, Sammy boy," said SpongeBob. "So did your mom!"

chapter four

Mr. Krabs stood glumly below the television set that was mounted on the wall of the Krusty Krab. His customers had demanded that *Mother Knows Best* be turned on every day, so they could watch it while they ate. On today's show SpongeBob was demonstrating how to remove stubborn pet stains.

"The boy's a natural at this stuff!" Mr. Krabs exclaimed to Squidward. "He's never coming back to work at the Krusty Krab. Look at that—me own mother is a fan!"

"Shhh!" said Mrs. Krabs, who was sitting at a table. "He's moving on to home decor!"

"SpongeBob, I need some color help!" said a member of the audience. "My walls are seafoam green and my sofa is medium sage. Any ideas for an accent color?"

"Why, sure," said SpongeBob. "My mother would probably suggest a soft floral rug with mauve or coral throw pillows."

"He's brilliant!" yelled Mrs. Krabs. "What an *eye* for color!" The other customers in the Krusty Krab nodded.

With a heavy sigh Mr. Krabs skittered into his office and closed the door.

Back at the studio Sam Sandollar thrust a piece of paper into SpongeBob's hands just as the show ended.

"Look at these ratings!" he said in a giddy voice. "The advertisers are all thrilled!"

He pulled SpongeBob into the conference room, where the decision makers sat waiting for him.

A loud cheer went up when SpongeBob entered the room.

"You're terrific!" gushed one of them. "I never thought I could learn so much about cleaning my bathtub!"

"I had my doubts about you," said another, "but you proved me wrong. And thanks to you, I make sure to call my mommy every day!"

The rest of them nodded.

"I'm sure glad you all enjoy the show," said SpongeBob. "But I really can't take any credit. I owe it all to—"

"MOM!" everyone gleefully shouted.

chapter five

SpongeBob sat in his dressing room while an assistant worked away at powdering his face. Patrick lounged on a nearby sofa eating a chocolate ice-cream cone.

Sam Sandollar dashed into the dressing room. "We're doing a show on soufflés today," he said anxiously to SpongeBob. "Have you made one of those before?"

SpongeBob laughed. "Piece of cake! I've

seen my mother make them millions of times!"

"Great," said Sam, heaving a sigh of relief. "And after the soufflé there's going to be a question-and-answer session with the audience on helpful household hints. Sound good?"

"Not to worry," said SpongeBob easily. "My mom taught me everything there is to know about helpful household hints."

Just as Sam was hurrying out, he remembered something. "Oh, right. Speaking of mothers . . . here's a letter from yours." He handed SpongeBob an envelope before heading out the door.

"Open it and read it to me, would you?" SpongeBob asked Patrick as the assistant began brushing his eyelashes.

Patrick tore it open and unfolded the note. Several drops from his ice cream dripped onto it and blocked out some of the words. Patrick read SpongeBob the note, skipping over the words he couldn't make out.

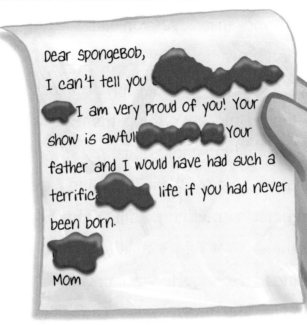

Dear SpongeBob,
I can't tell you ⬛⬛⬛
⬛ I am very proud of you! Your show is awful⬛⬛⬛ Your father and I would have had such a terrific⬛ life if you had never been born.
⬛
Mom

But what the note really said was:

Dear SpongeBob,

I can't tell you enough how proud I am—I am very proud of you! Your show is awfully wonderful! Your father and I would have had such a terrifically dull life if you had never been born.

Love,

Mom

After Patrick had finished reading the letter, SpongeBob sat up in his chair. He waved away the makeup assistant, who hurried out of the dressing room. SpongeBob's eyes began to well up with tears. His lower lip started to quiver. He turned to Patrick and said in a very small voice, "It sounds like my mom is not proud of me anymore!"

Patrick nodded solemnly. "It, uh, looks that way," he said. "That's too bad. I thought you said she loved you. I'm sorry, SpongeBob."

SpongeBob turned to look in the mirror. A stricken face looked back. "A mother's love is all that matters in life," he said slowly. "If I don't have that, life is meaningless."

He looked out the window. Outside he could see plenty of mothers who seemed to care deeply for their children. One mother was wiping her baby's nose with the hem of her skirt. Another mother was buying a shiny, new toy car at a toy store. And another mother was pushing a stroller quickly in the direction of the Krusty Krab, which displayed huge signs saying "Mother's Day Special! Double the price, double the goodness!"

"Why, who cares about soufflés anyway?"

said SpongeBob. "My mom is not proud of me!" And with those words he burst into loud, gushing sobs. Tears flew off his face so fast, the dressing room floor quickly flooded.

chapter six

"Okay, SpongeBob, it's magic-time!" yelled Sam Sandollar, poking his head into SpongeBob's dressing room. But what he saw was a sobbing SpongeBob.

"What's going on?" he asked.

"SpongeBob's mom is not proud of him," said Patrick, shaking his head sadly.

"But . . . but . . . you're doing a show on soufflés in four minutes!" said Sam. "SpongeBob, you have to pull yourself together!"

"Who cares about an old soufflé at a time like this!" wailed SpongeBob. "It's no use! What's the point if my mother isn't proud of me!" He sobbed even harder.

"Come on, SpongeBob!" Sam pleaded. "Keep it together, man! The show must go on!" He thought desperately for a way to convince SpongeBob. Finally he said, "SpongeBob, if you do a bad show, then *my* mom won't be proud of *me*! You don't want that, do you?"

SpongeBob stopped sobbing. He rubbed his eyes and blew his nose. "Okay," he said in a sad voice. "I'll do my best."

But the show was a disaster. The soufflé did not rise. Then during the question-and-answer session a member of the studio audience asked SpongeBob what to do about stubborn stains around her bathtub.

"Why bother?" said SpongeBob. "Who cares if you have a few stains?"

The audience gasped.

"SpongeBob," said someone else, "I can't get my little Timmy to make his bed. What do you suggest?"

"What's the point of making his bed?" said SpongeBob. "It just gets messed up again." SpongeBob let out a long sigh.

The people in the audience grew very quiet. Then troubled whispering began. A few people stood up and walked out.

Up in the control room Sam was having a fit. "What is the matter with him?" he shouted.

"Can you blame the poor guy?" said one of the technicians. "His mom said she's not proud of him anymore!" The others shook their heads sadly.

Sam's cell phone started ringing. "That's going to be the advertising sponsors," he moaned. "They'll be furious!"

The next day's show was even worse. Cakes

fell. Knitting unraveled. Stubborn stains refused to come out. Sam watched in horror as the show's ratings zoomed downward.

"What should I do?" he said to himself. "The show will be cancelled. Another flop! They'll fire me! My career will be ruined!" He sank into a chair and stared at the ratings chart.

And then a thought struck him. "I know!

I'll ask *my* mother what to do! After all, it was SpongeBob who taught me that valuable lesson: Mothers know best!"

Sam grabbed his cell phone and speed-dialed his mother.

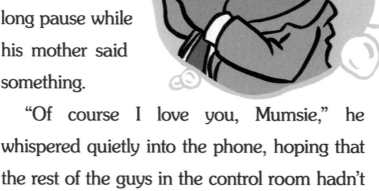

"Mother!" he said. "I have a really huge problem!"

There was a long pause while his mother said something.

"Of course I love you, Mumsie," he whispered quietly into the phone, hoping that the rest of the guys in the control room hadn't heard.

A few of them snickered and pointed, but he ignored them.

"I assume you have been watching the show recently? You have? I know, I know! SpongeBob is sad. He says his mom told him she's not proud of him. I've got to do something before my career is ruined. Mumsie, what should I do?"

There was a long pause while his mom said something. Sam kept saying "uh-huh, uh-huh" and nodding excitedly. Then finally he said, "Mumsie, that's a terrific idea. You always know what to do."

chapter seven

If it were possible for SpongeBob's show to get any worse, it did. The next day SpongeBob sat dully in front of the camera. He was supposed to be doing a show called "What to Make for that Special Mother for Mother's Day."

"Unlike me, maybe *you* have a mother who is *proud* of you," he said. "If I thought my mom cared, I would make her a hat out of a margarine tub for a Mother's Day present, like this." He sniffed a little bit, and held up a margarine tub. But the energy just wasn't there. Members of the audience were starting to look at their watches and to nod off to sleep. Someone coughed.

"Leave it plain," said SpongeBob. "or else, stick stuff on it like this." He sighed. "She might like it," he continued in a monotone, "but then again, she might tell you she's not proud . . . huh?" Something offstage had caught SpongeBob's eye.

Suddenly SpongeBob's mother stepped onto the set. All the TV cameras swiveled toward her, and then hurriedly swiveled back to record SpongeBob's surprised expression.

"Mom?" SpongeBob said weakly.

"SpongeBob!" said his mother, opening her arms. "My dear, dear boy! Oh, how proud I am of you!"

SpongeBob looked at her, his mouth open in astonishment. "But . . . but . . . your letter!" he stammered.

"I will always be proud of you," she said as SpongeBob's eyes filled with tears. He sprang up from his chair and flew toward his mother's waiting arms. The two embraced as the audience erupted in cheers. So did everyone in the control room. So did all the advertising sponsors sitting at the conference table. In fact, everyone watching the show in Bikini Bottom cheered!

Even Squidward, who had been watching the show from behind the cash register, quickly wiped away a tear.

The only one in Bikini Bottom who was not happy was Mr. Krabs. Inside his office, where he, too, had been watching the show, he let out a long moan. "Aaaaargh! Now SpongeBob will *never* come back to work here at the Krusty Krab!"

He skittered out of his office and into the dining area toward his mother. "What's wrong, Eugene?" she said to Mr. Krabs.

"SpongeBob's show is doin' great again," he said. "I'm afraid I've lost him forever as my fry cook. The place just . . . just isn't the same. What should I do?"

Mrs. Krabs looked thoughtful. "Go and tell him you want him back!" she said. "Sometimes all it takes is a kind word. As every mother will

tell you, a little word of appreciation goes a long way!"

"It's worth a try," said Mr. Krabs.

Back on the set of *Mother Knows Best*, SpongeBob and his mother were demonstrating how to make perfect ice cubes time after time. When Mrs. SquarePants cracked open the perfectly formed cubes, the audience gave her a standing ovation.

As soon as the show ended, Sam Sandollar ran out of the control room to shake hands with SpongeBob and his mother.

"I knew you would pull yourself together, SpongeBob!" he said.

SpongeBob looked over at his mother lovingly, then turned to Sam. "Like I told you once before," he said, "anything is possible with a mother's love!"

"How right you are, SpongeBob. How right you are," Sam agreed.

As SpongeBob and his mother were getting ready to leave, SpongeBob suddenly noticed Mr. Krabs.

"Hi, Mr. Krabs!" yelled SpongeBob.

"Hello, SpongeBob," said Mr. Krabs without enthusiasm.

"Hey, Mr. Krabs, why are you so sad?" SpongeBob asked.

Mr. Krabs sighed. "Well, SpongeBob, the truth is that the Krusty Krab just isn't the same without you," he said. "We do miss our fry cook, 'tis a fact. Won't ya please come back to work at the restaurant?"

"Gee, you really miss me?"

SpongeBob asked. He looked at Mr. Krabs's sad face, then turned to his mother and whispered something to her. She whispered something back.

"Well, if you miss me that much," said SpongeBob to Mr. Krabs, "then I'll come back to work for you!"

"Ya will?" yelled Mr. Krabs. "That's great! And just to show ya how glad I am to have ya back, yer mom gets free refills on ice water for Mother's Day!"

"Aw, gee, Mr. Krabs. You're too good to me," SpongeBob said.

"Hold on! Hold on!" said Sam, who had overheard the conversation. "What about your show, SpongeBob? It's a huge hit! The ratings are through the roof! You can't quit now!"

SpongeBob turned to him and smiled.

"I think I know the perfect someone who could take over for me, sir," he said.

"You do? Who?"

"Why, *you*, sir! Remember, you have a mother's love, and with that, anything is possible!"

"Gee, I never thought of it that way," Sam replied. "Maybe Mumsie and I could host the show together! What a terrific idea!"

He rushed off to call his mother.

"It sure is nice to have you back, SpongeBob," said Mr. Krabs, when he and SpongeBob got back to the Krusty Krab.

"It sure is nice to *be* back!" SpongeBob agreed. He put on his fry-cook hat and clipped on his name tag.

Suddenly Mr. Krabs was all business again. "You can start by swabbin' the decks and refillin' the ketchup dispensers!" he ordered.

"Yes, sir!" said SpongeBob with a salute.

"Oh, but before you do that, I have one little thing I want you to do first," said Mr. Krabs.

"What's that, Mr. Krabs?"

"Could ya show me how ta make one of dem adorable little hats out of a margarine tub?"

"Sure thing, Mr. Krabs!" SpongeBob said with a laugh.

about the author

Sarah Willson is the author of more than one hundred children's books. She lives in Connecticut with her husband, three children, and two cats. Sarah has never hosted her own television show, but she *was* on TV once (for about forty-five seconds) when she was in fourth grade, for winning an art contest.

Sarah has very fond memories of her own mother, who taught her how to cook. Her mom also tried to teach her how to knit and sew, but that didn't work out so well. Now that she is a mother herself, Sarah hopes she is modeling qualities like patience, understanding, and tolerance in her own children. But if they want to learn to sew and knit, they'll have to take a course or something.